ODYSSEUS AND THE ENCHANTERS

Retold by Catherine Storr
Illustrated by Mike Codd

Raintree Childrens Books
Milwaukee • Toronto • Melbourne • London
Belitha Press Limited • London

First published in the United States of America 1985
by Raintree Publishers Inc.
330 East Kilbourn Avenue, Milwaukee, Wisconsin 53202
in association with Belitha Press Ltd, London.

Conceived, designed and produced by Belitha Press Ltd,
2 Beresford Terrace, London N5 2DH

Library of Congress Cataloging in Publication Data

Storr, Catherine.
    Odysseus and the enchanters.

    Summary: Recounts the adventures of Odysseus as he encounters
Circe, the Sirens, and other dangers on his long voyage home from
the Trojan War.
    1. Odysseus (Greek mythology)—Juvenile literature. 2. Sirens
(Mythology)—Juvenile literature. [1. Odysseus (Greek mythology)
2. Mythology, Greek] I. Homer. Odyssey. II. Title.
BL820.03S76   1985   292'.13   85-12448
ISBN 0-8172-2502-1 (lib. bdg.)
ISBN 0-8172-2510-2 (softcover)

Far away in the seas around Greece lay a small island covered with thick forests. Men told strange tales about it.

"Sailors who land there are never seen again," said one old man.

"Nonsense! My son was there once and he saw lions and wolves roaming the woods. They looked wild, but when they saw my son they stood on their hind legs like men," said another man.

O dysseus, the cleverest of the Greek heroes, was sailing back after the Trojan War to rocky Ithaca, his kingdom. When he and his men reached the mysterious island, they were exhausted, after escaping great dangers.

For two days, they lay on the beach, getting back their strength. On the third day, Odysseus took his spear and his sword and climbed the cliffs to see what the island was like.

He reached the top of a hill from which he could see the whole island. From among the thickly planted trees, he saw a wisp of smoke rising into the clear air. He went back to the shore, carrying meat for his hungry companions, and that night they ate and drank and were refreshed.

The next morning, Odysseus divided the ship's company into two parties of twenty-two men in each. They cast lots, and it fell to Eurylochus, one of the officers, to take his party of men to explore the island. Odysseus and the others stayed on the shore.

Eurylochus and his men climbed the hill and they, too, saw the smoke rising from among the trees. As they approached, they saw a beautiful palace in a clearing of the forest. From the open windows of the palace came the sound of someone singing a sweet song. They were astonished to see the palace surrounded by mountain wolves and lions who came toward them, wagging their tails in a friendly way. The sailors ran for safety toward the palace. The doors opened, and a beautiful woman stood there and invited them to come in.

Almost all the men followed her into the palace. Eurylochus was the only one who stayed outside, fearing that this might be a trap. He looked through a window and saw Circe, the witch-goddess, give the men a sweet drink, mixed with a drug which made them forget their country, their wives, their children. Then she touched them with her wand, and drove them to the pigstyes. For each one had become a pig, with pigs' bristles and a pig's snout. They could not speak; they could only grunt.

Eurylochus was horrified. He rushed back to the shore to tell Odysseus. Odysseus took his sword and his bow and set off alone toward Circe's palace.

As he went, he saw a beautiful young man in his path. The young man took his hand and said, "Odysseus, do not look for your companions here. Circe, the witch-goddess, has penned them into her styes, like swine. She will do the same for you if you do not do exactly what I tell you. I am going to give you something that will keep you safe from Circe's magic. When she tries to turn you, too, into a pig, draw your sword and threaten to kill her. Make her promise to release your companions and not to try any more of her tricks."

The young man bent down and picked a little plant. Its petals were milk-white and its root was black. He said, "This herb is called Moly, and it will protect you. It is difficult for men to dig up, but we gods can do anything."

Then Odysseus knew that this was no ordinary man, but Hermes, the messenger of the gods.

As Odysseus approached Circe's palace he heard the witch-goddess singing at her loom. He called out, and Circe came to the door and welcomed him, as she had his companions. She led him in, and gave him a rich drink in a golden bowl. Then she touched him with her wand and said, "Go and join your friends in the sty."

But the herb Moly protected Odysseus, and he remained in his own shape, as a man. He drew his sword as if he meant to kill Circe.

17

Circe fell to her knees. "Who are you?" she cried. "Do not kill me! Stay here in my palace, and trust me, and learn to love me!"

But Odysseus remembered the warning of Hermes. He made Circe promise to turn his friends back into men, and to play no more tricks. Then her maids bathed Odysseus in warm water, and clothed him in a fresh tunic and cloak. They set before him and Circe fine food on silver plates and sweet wine in golden goblets.

Odysseus turned away. "I cannot eat or drink while my companions are still spell-bound," he said.

Then Circe went to the styes and drove out the herd of pigs. She smeared each beast with a magic balm, and as she did this, the pigs' bristles fell off, their snouts disappeared, and Odysseus saw his dear companions once more. He wept for joy.

Then Circe said, "Odysseus, go down to the shore and drag your ship high on the beach. Then bring the rest of your ship's company back here and stay with me for a while."

Odysseus did as Circe had asked. Then he and all the ship's company remained in Circe's palace for many months, feasting and singing, and living in soft delight.

At the end of a year, when they were leaving, Circe warned Odysseus of the dangers that still lay ahead. She told him of the Sirens whose song lured men to death. She told him of the horrible monsters, Scylla and Charybdis, and how to escape from them.

Odysseus said goodbye to Circe and he and his companions sailed away from her island. When they were nearing the island of the Sirens, Odysseus did as Circe had advised him. He knew that if his sailors heard the Sirens' song they would sail toward the island and every man would be lost. He softened a ball of wax, and with this he plugged the ears of every man but himself. He had told Eurylochus to bind him with ropes to the mast, and not to loosen the ropes, however much he pleaded.

As the ship came near the island, the Sirens sang an entrancing song. The sailors could not hear it, but Odysseus heard it and was filled with longing to go nearer, to land on the island and to taste the pleasures promised in the song. He pleaded with Eurylochus to untie the ropes; he ordered and he threatened. But Eurylochus only tightened his bonds and would not set him free until they were beyond the reach of the Sirens' song.

Now the ship came into the narrow channel that lay between Scylla and Charybdis. The men could already see the spray and churning water and hear the roar of the whirlpool, Charybdis, as she sucked the water down under the rocks on her side. On the other side they saw Scylla, a monster with six heads, grinning teeth, and twelve grasping feet which she dangled out of her cave, high on the rocks opposite Charybdis.

R ow as quickly as you can," Odysseus cried to the oarsmen. "Steer straight on, but keep nearer to Scylla, for if the whirlpool catches us, we shall all be lost," he said to the helmsman.

So the ship sped on, swift as a bird, between the two dangers. But the sailors were not quick enough. With her cruel feet, Scylla snatched up six of the men and crammed them into her six long-fanged mouths. Odysseus and the others wept for pity and fear, but now the ship was through the channel and had come out on to the open sea.

So Odysseus continued his journey, knowing he must face many more dangers. For Poseidon, the god of the sea, had sworn that it would take Odysseus ten years before he reached rocky Ithaca.